This book belongs to:

....

....

THE MAGICAL NAMING OF NANNA STRAWBERRY
...and a visit to the seaside

Author: Audrey Wilson 2016
Published by: Audrey Wilson 2017
e-mail: nannastrawberrystories@gmail.com
web: Blog: http://nannastrawberrystories.blogspot.co.uk/
telephone: 07514333705

Design and illustrations: Vladislava Vatashka 2017
https://www.behance.net/Vatashka

Logo courtesy of Michelle Smythe

ISBN 978 1 9998 112 0 4

Printed in Liverpool, England by PRINTFINE
RE-IMAGINING PRINT

Copy to The British Library

Introduction

I am an 81 years old mother of three (son and two daughters) grandmother of nine (3 grandsons 6 grand-daughters) and now great-grandmother of two, with another on its way to join our happy family. Added by them, one daughter in law, two sons in law, two grandsons in law, and some partners. I am proud of them all.

I love my new name, 'Nanna Strawberry' bestowed on me by my first great grandchild, Sophie, in 2015, she could not say Audrey. Becoming 'Nanna Strawberry' inspired me, at age 80, to write about 'The Magical Naming of Nanna Strawberry ...and a visit to the seaside' followed by eleven more stories also written at age 80. Each one is based on a special day shared with the children in my life over time. I invite readers to add their own special memories in telling the tale.

The next book will be 'Nanna Strawberry Makes a Badge ...and has tea with Sophie'.

Acknowledgements

My grateful thanks to everyone who read the draft manuscripts and offered positive comments which encouraged me to publish them. Also to everyone who enabled me to publish them! Especially to Vladi who I discovered by chance and who has completed excellent illustrations to stimulate the imagination of any child, creating fun from facts.

Dedication

To all the wonderful children in my life
and in the world!

Nanna Strawberry Stories

The Magical Naming of
NANNA Strawberry
...and a visit to the seaside

Book 1

©Audrey Wilson Author and Publisher

When Nanna Audrey looked out of her window and saw a clear blue sky and bright sunshine, she made a telephone call to her grand-daughter Emma.

'Would you like to bring Sophie for a day out at New Brighton today? It is such a lovely day and being near the seaside would be fun.'

'That is a nice idea Nanna' said Emma, 'we would love to come. See you soon.'

'Wear jackets, the sea breezes may be cool.'

When Emma and Sophie arrived hand in hand at Nanna's front door, carrying red beach buckets in their other hands, Sophie looked anxiously at her.

Emma said 'Nanna, Sophie is worried. She calls you "Nanna Strawberry" because she cannot say your name Audrey.'

'Oh' exclaimed Nanna,
'I think 'Nanna Strawberry' is a wonderful name!
I like it very much. Thank you Sophie.'

And so from that magical moment she became
'Nanna Strawberry'
to her happy gleeful great grandaughter.

Sophie beamed with pride.

'Leave your car on the driveway Emma,
we can take the bus to the ferry. The stop is just
across the road.'

The bus soon came. Sophie was very excited when
it arrived at their bus stop.
"Nanna Strawberry!"

Only Emma needed to pay for a ticket
Sophie was two and Nanna had a free Bus Pass.

Sophie enjoyed looking through the bus window,
pointing at passing houses and shops.

She often loudly called out
                    "Nanna Strawberry"
just to make Mummy and Nanna laugh.

The last stop was for the ferry across the River Mersey.
'Careful now, while we cross this busy road',
said Nanna Strawberry, 'Over to the Ferry Terminal.
Only Emma has to pay.'

'Not me, Nanna Strawberry, I am two' said Sophie,
nodding her head, remembering.

'And I have a free bus pass' laughed Nanna.

There were lots of people waiting for the ferry boat.
Emma pointed, saying 'Look,
It is sailing towards us, across the river.'

Noisy seagulls followed.

Excited Sophie shrieked "Nanna Strawberry".

A flag waved cheerfully at the front of the
brightly painted ferry boat.
It caused waves and white froth on the river,
Its engines were very noisy when it stopped.
Crewmen threw ropes to secure it. Then they
untied a heavy wooden ramp which clanged down to
make a footbridge on to the ferry.

The ferry boat was named 'Snowdrop'.
It was a great adventure walking aboard.
Emma carried Sophie up stairs to the open top deck
to a raft seat where they could watch the river and
swooping screeching seagulls while 'Snowdrop'
sailed back to Seacombe.
They waved their arms to the tuneful sound of
'Ferry Across The Mersey' when played by the crew.

When Nanna brought drinks, Sophie loudly called
"Nanna Strawberry". So proud she was able to say
Nanna's name properly! A bus from Seacombe
took them to the seaside at New Brighton.

They had crispy fish and chips at a café,
seated at an outside table so they could
enjoy the sunshine and view.

'Look' said Nanna, 'see the fort and
lighthouse across the road, next to the beach.
We can hear the fairground too, along the road.
The sand is hidden by seawater, which will soon
ebb away in the outgoing tide.'

Seagulls made a great noise, spreading
their wings to swoop down
for dropped chips.

Sophie held Nanna Strawberry's hand along
the promenade, Mummy carried bags,
passed the Fort, to a ramp down to the
shiny wet beach with puddles left by seawater.

Nanna Strawberry told Sophie.
'It will soon dry in the warm sun.'

Sophie sat on a low wall with Nanna, who asked a
friendly boy to collect seashells in Sophie's bucket.
Some children played ball games.

They watched Emma make sand pies with her bucket.
Sophie giggled while she kept loudly calling
          "N a n n a   S t r a w b e r r y"
knowing it always made Mummy and Nanna laugh.

All too soon Mummy Emma said
'Time to go home.'

This time, the ferry boat was named 'Royal Iris'. When sailing across the river Sophie was excited to see big birds on a roof top at the Pier Head. It was fun to watch 'Royal Iris' being tied up at the landing stage before its passengers could go ashore.

'Look Nanna Strawberry' called out Sophie.

Soon they were on another big bus, back to Nanna Strawberry's house.

Emma fastened Sophie into her car seat then started to drive away.

'Thank you, Nan, for a lovely time in New Brighton.'

'Thank you too, Emma and Sophie' said Nanna.

'Goodbye Nanna Strawberry' called out Sophie in her happy gleeful voice, waving from the car.

Nanna Strawberry gave a big smile and waved back. She was very happy with her new name. 'NANNA STRAWBERRY'! She liked it very much. Clever little Sophie for thinking of it.

Add your own story:

30

NANNA STRAWBERRY STORIES

Published 2017 - 2018

Anecdotal stories for children, lovingly written, beautifully illustrated.
Age 3 to 80+.

Published 2017

The Magical Naming of Nanna Strawberry ...and a visit to the seaside

Nanna Strawberry Makes a Badge ...and has tea with Sophie

Nanna Strawberry Goes Horse Riding ...and enjoys a happy birthday

Nanna Strawberry shares Christmas with an Angel

and in 2018

Nanna Strawberry Remembers Billy ...Joan's strawberry roan

Nanna Strawberry Remembers Shetland Pip ...and his young riders

Nanna Strawberry Remembers Crab Fishing ...and the Fun Machine

Nanna Strawberry Remembers Key Fishing ...and heroic Grandad

Nanna Strawberry Remembers the Young Queen ...and school

Nanna Strawberry Remembers Easter Fun ...and roll an egg

Nanna Strawberry Tells Stories to Sophie ...and meets her baby sister

Nanna Strawberry Goes to a Wedding ...and bakes a cake